MW01003003

BAREFOOT BOOKS

The barefoot child symbolizes the human being whose natural integrity and capacity for action is unimpaired. In this spirit, Barefoot Books publishes new and traditional myths, legends, and fairy tales whose themes demonstrate the pitfalls and dangers that surround our passage through life; the qualities that are needed to face and overcome these dangers; and the equal importance of action and reflection in doing so. Our intention is to present stories from a wide range of cultures in such a way as to delight and inspire readers of all ages while honoring the tradition from which the story has been inherited

THE
BIRDS WHO FLEW
BEYOND TIME

by

ANNE BARING

with pictures by

THETIS BLACKER

BAREFOOT BOOKS

BOSTON & BATH

We would like to acknowledge our debt to the translations of *The Conference of the Birds* by C. S. Nott (Shambhala, Boston, 1993) and Afkham Darbandi and Dick Davis (Penguin, London, 1984), and also to Diane Wolkstein and Samuel Noah Kramer for the four lines beginning "In the first days, in the very first days," translated from the Sumerian poem "The Huluppu-Tree" in their book *Inanna, Queen of Heaven and Earth* (HarperCollins, London, 1983).

We would also like to express our deep gratitude to our publisher, Tessa Strickland, and to Andrew Harvey for their inspiration, encouragement, and help in editing *The Birds Who Flew Beyond Time*.

The Birds Who Flew Beyond Time is dedicated to Farid ud-Din Attar. We are aware of the infinite preciousness of *The Conference of the Birds* and wanted to make its wisdom and radiance available to children all over the world.

The majority of the pictures were painted for a series called *The Search for the Simurgh* in 1981, which illustrated *The Conference of the Birds*. We are grateful to the many and various owners of these words for agreeing to their being used in this related but different context. The photographs are by Mark Fiennes, with the exception of the frontispiece, which is by John Challis.

We are grateful to ICI for providing the Procion Cold Dyes with which all the pictures in this book have been made.

BAREFOOT BOOKS

the children's books imprint of

Shambhala Publications, Inc.

Horticultural Hall

300 Massachusetts Avenue

Boston, Massachusetts 02115

Text © 1993 by Anne Baring

Illustrations © 1993 by Thetis Blacker

First published in Great Britain in 1993 by Barefoot Books Ltd

First published in the United States of America in 1994 by Shambhala Publications, Inc.

ISBN 1–56957–907–5

9 8 7 6 5 4 3 2 1

Distributed in the United States by Random House, Inc.,

and in Canada by Random House of Canada

Printed in Belgium by Proost International Book Production

A Note on *The Birds Who Flew Beyond Time*

The greatest myths, stories, and fairy tales are borne like seeds across the generations, taking root in a few individuals and bringing inspiration and soul-nourishment to many. These stories suggest responses to the challenges of human existence that cannot be conveyed as simply or profoundly in any other form. They carry us with them by enchantment. Through delight, they relate us to a dimension of the imagination too often neglected in our everyday lives.

The Birds Who Flew Beyond Time is inspired by the great Persian poem *The Conference of the Birds* written by Farid ud-Din Attar, a poet and Sufi mystic who lived in north-east Iran in the twelfth century. The central theme in Attar's poem – the need to awaken the heart – is as relevant and vital today as it was then.

Our story begins with an appeal for help by the Earth to all the birds of the world. She asks them to go on a special quest to save her life and describes the place they must reach in order to bring back a message for her from the Great Being who lives in the House of the Treasure in a garden beyond the edge of time. The Hoopoe comes forward and tells the birds that she knows the way and can act as their guide. She tells them the story of the Golden Feather that lies hidden in their hearts. Different birds come forward to express their doubts and fears but the Hoopoe persuades them to set out with her on the quest. She warns them that they will have to cross seven valleys, each one guarded by an invisible monster whose power must be overcome before they can find the garden of the Great Being. The birds then set out on their journey and after many trials, in which many of them succumb to the monsters' spell and must be left behind, they finally reach the garden beyond the edge of time. After explaining the purpose of their journey to the Keeper of the Gate, they are allowed to enter the garden and the House of the Treasure. The birds enter the Heart of the Great Being and ask what message they should take back to Earth. The Great Being tells them that they themselves are the message for, in breaking the spell of the seven monsters, they have been transformed from helpless, ignorant birds into birds capable of helping the Earth. The birds return to Earth through the seven valleys, rejoining their friends who, released from the monsters' spell, are free to fly home with them. They tell their story to the Earth who thanks them and appoints them as her special messengers to the children of the world.

The journey of the birds is everyone's journey through life; the Hoopoe is anyone's guide; the monsters represent the destructive powers of the wounded psyche, rigid and deadly in its uncomprehending pain. These destructive elements must be transformed before the soul is free to act on behalf of life. The Great Being is an image of the mystery that always transcends our intellectual grasp, yet which may be imagined, related to, and perhaps one day, when we least expect it, revealed.

A N N E   B A R I N G

THE BIRDS WHO FLEW BEYOND TIME

One day, the Earth was feeling very sad. She sent a message to her birds all over the world and said to them: "I need your help. Please will you gather together in one place so I can speak to you?"

So the birds came to listen to the Earth. They came from the north and the south, the east and the west. They flew secretly, at night, so that only children and night creatures would hear the whisper of their wings. As they flew, they called to each other and asked: "What does the Earth want? What can the Earth need? Why does she want to speak to us?"

At last they reached the place the Earth had named. It was a mossy glade in the midst of a forest. High above the trees a circle of snowy mountains glistened in the light of the full moon.

Here the birds settled with a great twittering and chattering. There were so many of them that their feathers touched each other and they looked at one another with interest and amazement. There were the great crested crane and the pink flamingo; the tiny, fragile hummingbird and the golden-crested wren from Africa; the bright parrot from South America; the tree sparrow from China. The arctic tern had flown many miles from the far north. The cormorant had come from the sea-shores and the wandering albatross from the wide oceans. The falcon, the eagle, and the great, gliding condor had come from the high mountains and from wild, desolate places. There were birds with strange faces, like the owl, and birds which sang beautifully, like the nightingale and the thrush; magical birds, like the paradise kingfisher and the fairy bluebird; and birds everyone knows, like the swallow.

There were hundreds of thousands of birds from everywhere on Earth. When the birds had told each other their names and the places they had come from, they ate and drank the food and water which the Earth had thoughtfully prepared for them. Then they settled down to listen to what the Earth had to say.

At first they heard a low rumble like distant thunder, and then from far, far away but so close that it seemed to come from inside their hearts, they heard a voice. It was very faint and weak and it spoke to them gently and lovingly, saying: "Be not afraid of me, my Birds. You have

been part of my life for millions of years and I have given you food and shelter during this long time. But now I need *your* help. With your wings you fly everywhere between earth and sky and with your eyes you see everything. You know more than people or animals because you are free to explore every hidden place. And so you know why I am sad.

"My great seas and rivers are filled with poisonous wastes which hurt the fish and the other small creatures that live in my waters; my tall forests are dying or are being cut down so I can no longer breathe properly. The clouds that are fed with moisture from my forests no longer gather and rain cannot fall from them to nourish me and all the creatures and plants I support. My sky is torn and the sun's burning rays injure me. My sea creatures – the whales and dolphins and turtles – are hunted and killed in my oceans and my animals are cruelly treated or destroyed. Poisons are buried deep in my body. These make me feel ill. If I am ill, I cannot grow food for all the life I love and the world will wither and die.

"In many places my people are killing each other, because they believe their part of the Earth belongs to them alone. They make weapons from my body to destroy each other. They tear my body apart with their bombs. Millions of children are hungry and hurt and dying because of these wars and they are taught to hate and fear each other as enemies. Few are those who can hear the voice of the Earth and listen to my cry for help. But you have seen all these things and you know them to be true. Will you help me?"

The birds set up a cry like a rushing wind: "What can we do to help the Earth?" they asked each other. "What does the Earth want?" Then together they asked the Earth: "How can we help you?"

The Earth spoke again. This time her voice was clear and strong: "Are you brave enough to go on a special journey to save my life? Are you clever enough to find the place that lies east of the sun and west of the moon, over the edge of time, beyond the seven valleys; the place that is neither here nor there but everywhere? Are you strong enough to break the spell of the monsters of the seven valleys? For my sake, will you dive to the depths of the sea that is unlike all other seas and look for the garden where there is a house with a hidden treasure? In that house there is a Great Being – one who is never old nor ever young, who is the life of all life. Speak to this Being. Say the Earth is in danger and has sent you for help. Then bring me back the message you are given."

The birds looked at each other in bewilderment. They had never heard the voice of the Earth before. They knew nothing about the Great Being over the edge of time beyond the seven valleys, and they had no idea how to reach the garden in the depths of the sea that was not like any other sea. Some of them thought the whole idea was a dream. Others said it was silly to expect birds from the Earth to fly so far away to find something which might not be there. Still others thought they might not have the strength for such a difficult journey and would die on the way. After a great deal of flying up and down and dusting of feathers and chattering, the Hoopoe flew into the center of the glade and settled on a small tree stump. The birds could see the fluttering of her black and white wings and the beautiful pink crest like a crown on her head. On her breast was a glowing ruby. On her long, curved beak were strange letters which the birds could not understand.

"Dear Birds," she began, "I am a messenger of the world invisible. I know the way to the garden beyond the edge of time. I have entered the House of the Treasure and seen the Great Being whom I serve and whose name is written on my beak. I can guide you to the place that is east of the sun and west of the moon. I have flown the lonely and dangerous way through the seven valleys to the treasure hidden in the depths of that sea which is unlike all other seas. I have seen through the hundred thousand veils of light and darkness that lie between us and the shining splendor of the Great Being. To make this journey you will need the courage of an eagle, the night vision of an owl, the wisdom of a raven and the gentleness of a dove." Then she told them a story.

"Long, long ago," she said, "in the first days, in the very first days, in the first nights, in the very first nights, in the first years, in the very first years, the Great Being who is the life of all life dropped a Golden Feather on the Earth. It was as delicate as a spider's web, as silken as a butterfly's wing and as radiant as a star. Every bird carried within its heart the same magical Golden Feather so that each was secretly linked to all the others and to the Great Being who gave it to the Earth. But soon, each bird made a picture of this feather and began to believe that his or her picture was different from every other bird's, and some began to think that theirs was special and better than anyone else's and so they began to quarrel with each other as to whose picture was best. They forgot the real feather hidden inside their hearts which linked them to each other and to the Great Being. They began to fight great battles with each other and forgot

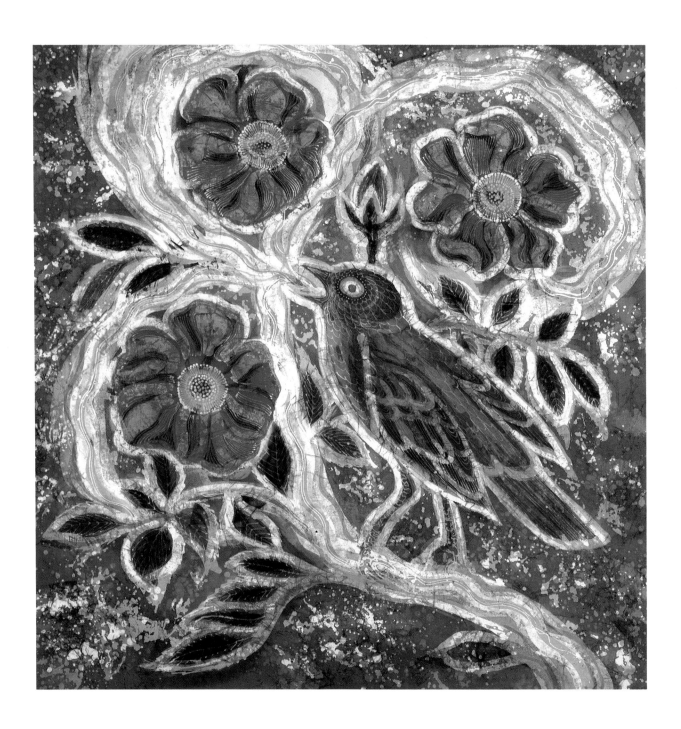

that they were all children of the Earth and that without the Earth they would die."

When the Hoopoe had finished, the birds began excitedly to discuss the Golden Feather and the journey to the Great Being. At first they decided they would all go together. But when they began to reflect on how long and difficult the journey might be, and on all they had to leave behind, they hesitated and, in spite of their good will, they began, one by one, to excuse themselves.

The nightingale said: "I love to sing all night long to the rose in the gardens of the world. If I go on this journey, the rose might die without my song. How could I leave her for a single night?"

The Hoopoe said: "What good will your singing be if there are no gardens left and no roses to fill them? Come with me to the garden of gardens and bring back the message for the Earth from the Great Being. Open your throat and sing to the birds as they face the dangers of the journey. Sing to them of trust and hope and courage and joy so they do not lose heart. Then you can sing for evermore to the roses in the gardens of the world."

Then, dressed in brilliant green with a ring of gold around her neck, the parrot spoke: "If I left the warm, moist jungles where I have lived for thousands of years, how would I survive in another kind of place? What is the point of making this journey when I may not be able to live in that garden, let alone find my way back?"

The Hoopoe replied: "Where will you live when your tall, rich forests are cut down? Where will you find a place to perch and to call to your friends on other trees? Why do you have so little trust in yourself and so little love for the Earth who has cared for you like a mother for so long?"

The peacock spoke next, splendidly arrayed in feathers of a hundred thousand colors. This way and that he turned, showing himself in all his glory to the assembled birds. "I think the Earth is exaggerating. I am an expert and know better than the Earth what is going on in the seas and forests, the deserts and cities of the world. This Great Being she talks of may be just a dream. There is no proof that what she says is true."

The Hoopoe said: "O foolish Peacock whose splendid dress hides a cold heart and a deaf ear. This is the first time the Earth has ever spoken to her birds. We do not need proof. We need to listen to her voice and trust our heart."

Then it was the turn of the duck: "I live in the water of ponds and rivers and in them I find my food. Clear water rushes down from the snowy mountains and hills of the Earth into the rivers that are my home. But the rivers are no longer bright and sparkling. Poisoned water from factories at their edge pours into them. The fish sometimes die and the water is no longer good for me. I will come with you for the sake of all the ducks and water birds in the world and for the sake of the Earth."

The Hoopoe said: "Thank you, Duck, for speaking up in this way. Your courage will give strength to others."

Now the partridge added his voice: "I have been injured in the wars that lay waste the Earth. My wife is dead, my children starving and homeless. My heart is burnt to ashes with hate for those who did these things. My only wish is for revenge so that others will suffer as I have suffered. Yet because of my pain I can understand the pain the Earth is feeling and I too will go with you to bring back a message from the Great Being to help her."

"This journey may heal your heart," said the Hoopoe.

Suddenly, the hawk, fierce and proud and dressed for battle, swooped toward the Hoopoe. His talk was always of armies, weapons, victory: "I don't know why you weep and wail about war. There has always been war and there always will be. It is necessary to kill one's enemies and to suffer in order to win. Why should I face the dangers of the way when there are more glorious battles to fight here?"

"You stain the Earth with blood," replied the Hoopoe. "Why not be a warrior for peace instead of for war? A warrior can protect life instead of destroying it. Is it not foolish to talk of war between birds when the life of the Earth herself is in danger? If you are as brave as your boast, come with us on this journey."

Then the tall, grey heron stepped forward: "I am so gentle that no one complains of me. I stand at the edge of the water, dreaming my dreams. I am too delicate for the journey you speak of."

The Hoopoe answered: "Dreams can take you away from your true path in life. Like the lakes and rivers, dreams may be gentle and pleasant but they may also overwhelm you like the raging flood waters. Come with us to the sea which contains all wonders, all treasures; then your dreams may come true."

Next the hummingbird spoke, feeble in body but tender in heart, trembling like a flame from head to foot. She said: "Do you think that a tiny bird like me, frail as a butterfly, could make her way to the garden of the Great Being? A hummingbird could never do it."

The Hoopoe answered her: "How do you know what you can accomplish unless you start out? Sometimes the weak have more courage and endurance than the strong. It is better to begin than to give up before the first trial. Take heart and join us; then what a story you will have to tell your children!"

The owl fluffed out her feathers and spoke: "I am a bird who was old before the Great Flood. I have witnessed many things since the beginning of time. It is too late for us, feeble birds that we are, to do anything. There is no point in trying. There are too few of us who care."

"Wise Owl, most respected of birds," said the Hoopoe, "it is never too late. Where danger is greatest, there is the greatest hope for change. The Earth has chosen *us* to help her. As she trusts us, can we not trust her? The choice you make can change the past and the future."

After all the birds had had their say, the Hoopoe spoke once more: "If you lose yourself in a glass of water, how will you dive to the depths of the sea beyond the edge of time? If you cannot light a tiny flame, how will you reach the blazing fire at the heart of life? If you have not the energy of an atom, how will you find the strength to help the Earth? For this quest you must have the heart of a lion."

The birds thought this over and again spoke to the Hoopoe: "It will be a miracle if we survive this journey. Could you tell us something about the Great Being who lives east of the sun and west of the moon, who is neither here nor there but everywhere? Then perhaps we would find the courage to set forth."

The Hoopoe replied: "O Birds without memory! You have forgotten the Golden Feather in your hearts which floats like a song on the breath of the Great Being. If you love the Earth as much as she has loved you, set out with fiery heart toward the goal, making that your greatest joy!"

Now the birds felt a change of heart. Their love for the Earth lifted them up; the idea of the Great Being beyond the edge of time filled their minds with wonder. Everyone trusted the Hoopoe because she was the messenger of the world invisible and knew the way to the garden and because the name of the Great Being was written on her beak. All the birds

listened as she spoke:

"We have seven valleys to cross and only after we have crossed them all shall we find the garden in the depths of the silver sea. Have courage and patience, Birds, and trust me to help you face the dangers of the way. We have to fly into a great darkness, the darkness of the seven valleys. Each valley is ruled by an invisible monster who lives inside a high mountain. Everything in the valley lies under its magic spell. Once, long ago, the monsters were one with the Great Being. But pain and fear came between them and separated them. They carry a great wound in their hearts and have forgotten who they are. Because they are wounded, they wound others. In their loneliness and pain they have become dangerous and terrible and as hard as stone.

"There are many ways of crossing these valleys and not all birds fly alike. We shall make the journey together but each must find his or her own path through the valleys. As you break the spell of the monster who rules each valley, you will discover skills you did not have before. You will become stronger and wiser and more loving. As you pass through the darkness a different kind of light will shine and will show you many things you could not see before. You will marvel at thousands of bright secrets. You will find your true friends."

At last the trembling birds set out. The first to follow the Hoopoe was the goldfinch, whose wings shimmered in the sunlight. After her came the fairy bluebird. All those who had spoken and more, many more, were there. So great was their number that the noise of their wings was like the roaring of waters in spring as they rush down the mountains toward the sea. As the birds left the Earth and flew toward the darkness of the seven valleys, they looked back and saw their home, shining in space like a precious jewel, and they wept because it was beautiful and they loved it and hoped to see it again.

Soon, they saw ahead of them the great darkness of the first valley, the Valley of Doubt. Panic spread among them and they huddled together, drawing in their heads and wings and wailing piteously. Some sank to the ground in bedraggled heaps and said they did not want to go on. One of them cried out: "We can't go on this journey. Our wings and feathers are not strong enough to carry us through this darkness and we are shaking with fear. We've never done anything like this before. If we fly into this valley, it is certain we will never find our way through it." And away they flew back to the Earth.

The rest crowded anxiously around the Hoopoe. Suddenly, the nightingale and the turtledove began to sing and they sang a melody so sweet that all who heard it were enchanted and once again took courage. They knew the task before them was mighty and the way was long and difficult but they were no longer so frightened. They felt they might be able to reach the garden in the depths of the secret sea.

The Hoopoe then said to them: "The magic spell of the Monster of Doubt fills the valley with a thick, gray fog which has the smell of stagnant water. This fog will ooze from the mountain and wrap itself round you, blinding you and making you lose your way. It will settle on your wings, and they will become wet and heavy so you can hardly fly. The invisible monster will confuse you with the soft whispering of its voice. At first you will not be able even to hear it, or know which direction it is coming from, but if you listen very carefully, you will hear these words sounding as if they were spoken by you, in your own voice: 'You are not good enough to find the treasure; you are not clever enough to break my spell; you are not strong enough to reach the garden; you will not survive this journey.'

"Do not listen to these whispers. They are not your own true voice but the voice of the monster who pretends to be you and will try to make you forget your own voice. Remember the clear music of the nightingale and the gentle song of the turtledove. Trust yourselves, for that is the magic that will break the spell of the Monster of Doubt. Remember the Golden Feather, radiant as a star in your hearts. It is the talisman that will protect you through all the dangers of the seven valleys."

The birds plunged bravely into the darkness of the first valley, the Valley of Doubt. At once, they were lost in a thick, murky fog that blinded them and weighed down their bright feathers. They smelt the smell of stagnant water. At first, they heard nothing at all and then, so faintly that it was like the fall of a leaf, came the soft, whispering voice of Doubt, speaking with their own voice: "You are not good enough to find the treasure; you are not clever enough to break my spell; you are not strong enough to reach the garden. You will never survive this journey."

But the birds remembered the Hoopoe's words. Even the quail, so hesitant and full of doubts, remembered. Beyond the monster's whisper, she heard the flute-like voice of the nightingale and the calm song of the turtle-dove. She remembered to trust herself and suddenly

saw the Golden Feather, clear as the sun, in her heart. She found her true voice and said to the monster: "You cannot fill me with the fog of doubt. I will not listen to your words. I am good enough, I am clever enough, I am strong enough to reach the Great Being. I will overcome the power of your spell." As she said these words, her wet, dragging wings grew lighter. Through the wisps of fog she clearly saw the Hoopoe flying in front of her and knew she had broken the spell of the Monster of Doubt. But a few birds could not tell the difference between their voice and the voice of the monster and their wings grew heavy and could not carry them through the valley.

The birds that remained flew on into the darkness of the second valley, the Valley of False Dreams. The air was thick and sweet and suffocating and soon they could not see their way. They heard the muffled voice of the monster, speaking from inside the mountain: "Follow me," it said, "and I will show you a quicker, easier way to the garden of the Great Being. Follow me and I will give you a special drink that will make you brave and strong. Come my way and I will give you dreams that will make you forget your fear and loneliness."

"Do not listen to this voice," cried the Hoopoe, "or you will fall into a deep sleep; do not drink what the monster offers you or you will forget who you are and your life will be lost!"

But the birds felt thirsty and weak after their journey through the Valley of Doubt. Invisible talons held out strange things for them to drink which smelt sweet and delicious. It seemed safe to taste them. The heron took a sip of the deadly drug. The Hoopoe's warning began to fade from his memory. He fought hard to stay awake, because the monster's spell was as strong as a magnet, but he was very weak and called to the other birds for help. Then he saw that they too were slipping away into sleep. He struggled desperately to reach them before it was too late. As he did so, a breath of clear, fresh air blew through the valley. Now the heron felt strong once more. With his long beak he tore the drink away from the other birds. He said to the monster: "We do not want your False Dreams. We will not stay in your valley. We love the Earth and want to help her. We love and trust ourselves and each other. We will not forget who we are." And he broke the spell of the monster and flew out of the valley. But some birds, who had drunk too much of the drug that tasted so sweet, forgot who they were and fell asleep in the Valley of False Dreams. And they were left behind.

Then the birds flew on, on into the darkness of the third valley, the Valley of Envy. At once they could feel the powerful spell of the monster of this valley. Each bird longed to be like some other bird. The hummingbird wanted to be strong like the eagle; the eagle wanted to be clever like the owl; the owl wanted to be beautiful like the peacock; the peacock wanted to sing like the nightingale; the nightingale wanted to be powerful like the hawk; and the hawk wanted to be more powerful than all the other birds put together. As these thoughts attacked them, they felt their feathers caught in the meshes of the monster's invisible nets, like the nets of the hunters they feared on Earth.

From inside the mountain, the monster's shrill voice mocked them, saying: "You are too helpless and too weak to break my spell. You will not free yourselves from the nets of Envy because they are as strong as iron." The birds thrashed and struggled in the nets, their wings torn and bruised and their beaks sore from pecking. Even the eagle panicked: "If only I could be like the condor," he cried. "If only I were stronger, faster, braver, I could free myself from these nets." Then, from far, far away, they heard the Hoopoe's faint voice: "Remember the feather in your hearts. Remember the Golden Feather, delicate as a spider's web, silken as a butterfly's wing, radiant as a star, which links you to each other and to the Great Being who is the life of all life. Let go of your wish to be someone else. Be true to yourselves and the nets of Envy will dissolve." The Hoopoe's voice startled them for, in their terror, they had forgotten all about her. As they remembered the Golden Feather in their hearts, the tiniest, weakest birds, the hummingbird and the wren, found a way to cut the threads of the nets and make holes so that the bigger birds could squeeze through them and fly free. But some birds had damaged their wings beyond repair and were unable to fly and they stayed in the valley. And the others who had to leave them behind wept with pity for their friends caught in the nets of Envy and wished they had been able to save them.

The birds who were free flew on into the darkness of the fourth valley, the Valley of Hate. From far away they saw a volcano belching fire from its cone. A wind like a tornado roared toward them. Flaming rivers of molten lava flowed down the sides of the mountain, burning everything in their path. The birds smelt the acrid stink of the monster's breath as its harsh cry exploded across the valley, and they trembled with fear: "No one can stand against me," roared the monster. "Where Hate rules, nothing lives. Your way lies through me and you will be burnt

to cinders as you fly."

But the birds, who were led by the partridge, trusted the Hoopoe and held to the course set by her. The heat of the monster's flames scorched the air and made them feel faint and sick as they drew nearer and nearer to the fiery mountain. Clouds of white-hot sparks raced toward them. The partridge gasped in pain as the sparks fell on his feathers but bravely he flew on through the searing fire. Although he had suffered terribly in the wars on Earth, he did not surrender to the spell of Hate. And his courage inspired all the other birds. "Are you still alive?" cried the Hoopoe. "Yes!" they chorused. "But our feathers are burnt and blackened." The Hoopoe encouraged them, saying: "If you have survived at all, you have broken the spell of the Monster of Hate. You are amazingly strong and brave birds to have come through this valley and many blessings will come your way." But some birds lay dead on the floor of the valley. And when the remaining birds saw them, they wept with sorrow for their friends who had died in the flames of Hate and wished they could bring them back to life.

Now the birds who had survived followed the Hoopoe into the darkness of the fifth valley, the Valley of Power. As they flew she told them that to overcome the spell of this monster they must be stronger than steel yet more gentle than the fairy bluebird. They saw a landscape as cold and empty as a dead planet, dried to a white powdery dust. Nothing green or living was to be seen. The air was so dry and thin that the birds gasped for breath. Fear, like an invisible iron hand, clutched at their throats. The monster's roar was like an avalanche and they heard it shout from the mountain top: "I control everything. I know the truth about everything. I am always right. If you stay in my valley, I will give you all the power, all the control, all the knowledge you want, so others will have to obey you. You will never again be weak, helpless, ignorant birds. You will never again need to suffer."

The birds hesitated. They began to feel paralyzed by the black, invisible rays of the Monster of Power. The peacock was unable to move. He tried to fan out his tail but could not do so. He felt his heart growing heavier and colder as if it were turning to stone.

"Wake up!" shouted the Hoopoe, as she flew frantically back and forth in front of him, trying to break the spell. "Wake up before it is too late and you have lost your heart for ever. The Monster of Power is very, very clever, like the Monster of False Dreams. It will persuade you to stay in this valley and forget your quest for the Great Being of the world invisible." The peacock

heard her voice as if it came from far away, at the bottom of the sea. He flapped his wings as hard as he could and jumped up and down. But on his own he could not break the spell of the Monster of Power and he cried aloud for help. At that moment, hundreds of tiny sparrows, ordinary little birds whom no one usually noticed, heard his cry and flew between him and the paralyzing ray of the Monster of Power. By their desperate efforts to save him, the peacock was freed from the terrible spell. But other birds could not resist the black rays of the monster. They were turned to stone and could not fly out of the valley.

Now the birds who were left approached the darkness of the sixth valley, the Valley of Cruelty. The Hoopoe warned them: "The spell of the monster who rules this valley is very strong and hard to see. You will have to find the courage to face your own cruelty."

"That will not be difficult," thought the hawk. "I am very brave."

As the birds flew into the Valley of Cruelty, wave after wave of winged creatures screamed out of caves in the mountain to attack them. Half bird, half demon, each was armed with cruel talons and stings as sharp as needles. Their venom poisoned the birds so that many fell to the ground as though dead. The birds shook with fear as they cowered before these winged creatures, for they did not know how to fight them. They heard a voice in their hearts saying: "It's all right to be cruel. It's fun to be cruel. It's brave to be cruel." The hawk realized he had never fought a battle like this one and would need every ounce of his courage and strength to face these creatures of Cruelty. Suddenly, he saw that some of them were the ghosts of birds he had killed in battle. He was face to face with his own cruelty which he had never seen before and hot tears streamed from his eyes. But because he was very brave, he called out to the monster of the valley: "I will not fight any more. Call off your creatures of death! Release them from your spell! Let me be friends with my former enemies. Killing only brings more death."

From inside the mountain, the monster answered him: "O Hawk, do you think one bird can break the spell of ten thousand years? What is your feeble will against mine? Do you think these demon birds will stop fighting because you invite them to be friends? You may be brave but you are a fool." But the hawk cried out: "I am now a warrior on behalf of life. I call upon the power of the holy name of the Great Being, and the names of all the birds of the Earth, to stand with me for life against death. Your spell is broken." Then all the birds gave a great shout and it shattered the mountain where the Monster of Cruelty lived, and the terrible spell of Cruelty was

broken for ever. But in the battle with the demon creatures, many thousands of birds had perished and their corpses littered the valley. From the mountain pass above the valley, the pheasant looked back at them and wept with grief. All at once he saw a golden heart glowing in the sky and knew that the love he felt for his friends lost in that battle would one day bring them back to life.

Then the few birds who had survived flew on, on into the darkness of the seventh and last valley – the Valley of Despair. The Hoopoe said: "Do not fall under the spell of the monster's voice speaking in your heart, for if you do, you will forget yourselves and die from fear. Listen carefully for the voice of the nightingale and look out for the ruby on my breast. Come, my valiant Birds; this is your last trial and the most difficult, for this monster has the deepest wound and is more terrible than all the others."

The birds could see nothing. The darkness was as black as a raven's wing. The monster's breath squeezed them like a python. It made them feel numb and cold and so weak and weary that they longed to die. The owl felt the power of the monster seize her like the tentacles of an octopus, pulling her deeper and deeper into an icy blackness colder than the coldest water she had ever felt on Earth. But she was stronger now for she had broken the spell of the other six monsters. She did not forget the Hoopoe's words and listened very carefully for the evil voice in her heart. Then she heard the monster, speaking with her own voice and saying over and over again: "You have failed the quest; your journey is useless. There is no point to anything. You will never leave this valley for there is nothing beyond it. Now you will never reach the garden. There is no garden. There is no treasure. There is no Great Being over the edge of time. There is no message to bring back to the Earth. You will disappear into darkness for ever."

The monster's voice made the owl feel sick with horror, but just as she felt herself on the verge of slipping into darkness, she heard the soaring voice of the nightingale ring out, clear and true: "I sing of joy and light and colour and beauty. I sing of the bliss of following the way of the heart through the seven valleys. I sing to help you defeat the spell of the Monster of Despair; I sing to help you trust yourselves, to help you remember, remember, remember joy."

And the Hoopoe cried aloud to all the birds: "Come on! Remember the Earth for whose sake you have traveled this far. Close your eyes and you will see a beam of white light, powerful as a laser, pouring into the valley from the garden of the Great Being. It is dissolving the

darkness. Follow this brilliant beam of light and you will break the spell of the last monster." And as she spoke, the ruby on her breast glowed like a pulsing heart in the darkness. And the birds, though nearly overpowered by Despair, remembered the Earth and their love for her. They closed their eyes and saw the bright beam of light. Led by the owl, they began to fly along it.

As they flew, they sang a song to the Monster of Despair. Each one found his or her true voice and sang a special song. Together the birds made a song of such power and wisdom and beauty that, in spite of itself, the monster fell under their spell. They sang of their love for the Earth and the beauty and wonder of life. They sang of their happiness because they were able to fly through the sky yet rest on the Earth. They sang of their trust in the Great Being who was the life of all life and they told the monster about the garden in the depths of the sea. As they sang, their fear vanished and the monster, who listened to every word, began to sing too. As it sang, the terrible wound in its heart was healed. Slowly, slowly, the birds saw the darkness dissolve and the light become stronger and stronger, until it was as bright as the sun at midday. And because the birds had healed the monster, none of them stayed behind in the Valley of Despair.

The healing of the Monster of Despair had given the birds new strength and courage. Even so, they wondered if they would be able to reach the garden and the Great Being over the edge of time. They hoped their journey would not take so long that they would be too late to save the Earth. And so, keeping close to each other for support and comfort, yet at the same time finding their own special way, they came at last to the edge of time and the shore of the great sea that is unlike all other seas. They were very frightened of diving into this sea for they thought they might die and never wake up. But the paradise kingfisher, gleaming in his brilliant blue-green plumage, said he knew how to dive into deep water and begged them to follow him without fear.

So, holding their breath, they dived to the depths of those silvery waters which reminded them of their dreams. The waters caressed them gently and the birds found that they were partly flying and partly swimming through this sea. It was neither as light as air nor as heavy as water, but clear as crystal, like dew in sunlight. As they went deeper and deeper, it lay like a cloud over their heads. All of a sudden, just as they felt they had reached the end of their strength and

could go no further, they saw the garden, shimmering and glimmering like an emerald at the bottom of the sea.

Of all the hundreds of thousands of birds who had started out on the journey, only a few reached the garden. Many had lost their feathers and their bodies were scarred with burns and cuts from their journey through the seven valleys. They could hardly recognize each other. They had just enough strength to lift their heads to look around them at the garden. The nightingale was the first to see that it was full of the most beautiful trees and flowers, including his beloved roses; roses fresher and more fragrant than any he had ever seen or imagined. He cried aloud in wonder to the others. The ground was soft with warm green moss and covered with wild strawberries. Cascades of flowers hung from the trees and their blossoms scented the air with delicious perfumes. Waterfalls sparkled and everywhere they heard the humming of bees as they gathered honey. In the middle of the garden was a mound and they saw a flight of steps leading up it to the House of the Treasure. The house was lit up as if the walls were transparent. A great light was shining inside it.

Suddenly, the door of the House of the Treasure opened and they saw a tall and majestic figure, dressed in a robe like a rainbow. It looked at the huddled birds and said with great tenderness: "Where have you come from, O Birds, and what are you doing here? What are your names? O you who have left everything behind you to follow the quest through the darkness of the seven valleys, where is your home? Why have you come here? What do you want and what can I do for you?"

Then the exhausted birds fluttered into life and spoke, their voices faint with awe: "Our guide, the Hoopoe, has led us here from the Earth far, far away. It has taken us a lifetime to reach the garden. We have come to bring a message from the Earth to the Great Being who is the life of all life. The Earth is very sad and she has sent us to ask for help. If we are not allowed through the door, what is there left for us to do? We cannot return to the Earth without bringing her the message from the Great Being."

Then the Keeper of the Door, having tested their hearts and found them true, gently invited them to enter the House of the Treasure. And now, as they climbed the steps, the birds began to tremble, for they stood at the threshold of the Majesty that no one can describe, that no one can imagine. On either side of them, flowers blossomed as they looked at them and filled the

air with heavenly perfumes. Overcome with joy and wonder, they saw in a blaze of glowing light, a radiant glory through the doorway of the House of the Treasure. There, before them, was the Great Being they had come across all the worlds to find.

The birds crossed the threshold of the House of the Treasure and entered the Heart of the Great Being. It was as if they entered a room of a thousand dazzling mirrors, each one reflecting a light so brilliant that at first they were blinded. Then, slowly, as their eyes grew accustomed to the light, they saw reflected in the mirrors the innermost secret of creation, light streaming into all the forms of life. As they gazed, lost in the splendor of their vision, they knew they were inside the Heart of the Great Being. And each of them knew they were, at one and the same time, themselves and each other. They were at once the Great Being and every single, tiny, shining particle of that life. In that instant, they saw through the hundred thousand veils.

They saw thousands of dancing suns each more glorious than the other, thousands of moons and stars all equally resplendent. They saw that each one was a universe and that all these worlds blossomed inside the Heart of the Great Being.

Then the voice of the Great Being spoke to them: "In the first days, in the very first days, in the first nights, in the very first nights, in the first years, in the very first years, when everything needed was brought into being by me, the life of all life, I gave to the Earth a Golden Feather, delicate as a spider's web, silken as a butterfly's wing, radiant as a star. I knew that after many millions of years that feather would bring you to me in the world invisible, to my garden in the depths of the sea. You listened to the Earth. You followed the Hoopoe, messenger of the world invisible, beyond the edge of time to find me at the heart of life. You have asked me for a message to take back to the Earth.

"You yourselves, as you are now, you are the message. You have broken the spell of the monsters of the seven valleys. You have seen the vision of the Treasure. You are no longer helpless, weak, ignorant birds. Now you know your true nature, the divine heart of your being. You know that I am the heart of each one of you and you are within my Heart for ever. Now you can return to the Earth knowing that every atom, every stone, every leaf, every tree of Earth is lit with the one secret, blazing light that streams from me.

"Wherever you are, you have only to imagine me and I will be with you. If ever you are anxious, I will give you strength and wisdom. If ever you are afraid, you have only to imagine my

ight and it will stand shining before you. You have flown beyond the edge of time so you know there is no death but only one eternal life. Tell all the children of the Earth what you have seen so they will not fear death. Go now, my beloved Birds, and tell your story to the Earth."

And the birds, with glorious new plumage, and with the Golden Feather shining in their hearts, set out for the Earth. The journey that had taken so long now flashed by in a second and they saw that each of the seven valleys had become as beautiful and richly alive as the garden. The land that had been frozen and blackened and poisoned and scorched by the monsters' spell was restored to life. And, best of all, the birds who had fallen under the spell of the monsters came alive and flew with their friends toward the Earth. Together they saw the jewel-like beauty of their home coming closer and closer toward them, until suddenly they were at the Meeting Place of the Birds. Once again they felt the mossy ground beneath their claws, but now it was strewn with flowers glowing like tiny stars. They were welcomed by all the birds who had not made the journey. Then, quietly, they told the Earth their story.

The Earth listened to them, and when they had finished, she said in a gentle voice: "Dear Birds, you have saved my life. How can I thank you for what you have done for me and all my life held under the spell of the monsters of the seven valleys? You are all my special messengers: tell your story to my children. If they listen to your voice in their hearts, they will know what to do for me. They will love and protect me for my sake and for the sake of their children and their children's children. They will not fall under the spell of the seven monsters. One day, each of them will make the journey to the garden in the depths of the sea. And you will be their guide as the Hoopoe was your guide. You will lead them to the House of the Treasure and the Great Being who is the life of all life. Like the Hoopoe, you now are the messengers of the world invisible, and the Golden Feather will shine for ever in your hearts."